I0741764

For the Nostalgic.

Release that strap of time betwixt and about your beckoning limbs. Squeeze the fumbling doubt of the now. Graze the airy null of the yon.

Title Page Art by:
Rich Perotta &
Amanda Rachels

writers
Kevin LaPorte
@kevinlaporte
Erica J. Heflin
@ericajheflin

logo designer
Nathan Smith
@nuttsmith73

letterer
Weston Design Studio
@weslocher

artist/cover artist
Rich Perotta
@artistrich1980
Assisted by Catherine Michetti

colorist/back cover artist
Vito Potenza
@PiwiTFP

SCISSOR SISTERS presented by INVERSE PRESS - 11101 Rachels Lane, Foley, AL 36535.

Entire Contents © Kevin LaPorte & Erica J. Heflin. 1st Printing - December, 2016.
ISBN 978-0-9863974-5-5

INVERSE

http://inversepress.com
facebook.com/inversepress
Twitter: @inversepress
Instagram: @inverse_press

EPISODE ONE

Grand Canyon, AZ.
2617.

THE STRONG BECAME POWERFUL.
THE WEAK BECAME THEIR SLAVES.

I AM AMONG THOSE WHO GROVEL IN THE
SANDS, EYES ON THE HEAVENS, DIRT ON OUR
BREASTS. WE TURN OUR SIGHTS TO THE STARS,
TO THE INDOMITABLE FUTURE, AND DREAM.

FOR, IN THE FUTURE,
WE SEEK HOPE.

AND WE DO
NOT FIND HER.

FOR IN THE STARS, CRUELTY IS
THE ONLY TRUE CONSTANT.

ASHLULTUM.
CIRCA 1590 B.C.

LONG BEFORE HISTORY WAS RECORDED AND ORAL
TRADITIONS WERE PASSED FROM PARENT TO CHILD,
COMMUNITIES WERE SHAPED AND GIVEN STRUCTURE.

I...I ASSURE YOU, THE SMITH IS PROPERLY MOTIVATED.
SHE WILL CONTINUE TO PAN THE STREAM. THERE IS NO TASK FOR WHICH SHE IS BETTER SUITED.
AND WHO BUT THE CONTINUUM COULD DELIVER HER TO DESTINY?
ALLOW ME TO SHARE MY QUALMS, M'LADY.
HER LATEST CREATION, CONSTANT. A GIFT FOR THE RELIGION COMMITTEE.
KINKY. OUR SMITH IS A WOMAN OF INCOMPARABLE EXPERTISE.

WHAT SAY YOU, REVEREND GOODFELLOW? ARE ANY OF YOUR KIN WORTHY OF SUCH A BOON FROM QUEEN MAKEDA?
WELL? WHO HAS GOD SHONE HIS HOLY LIGHT ON THIS DAY?
IS IT YOU, REVEREND? NO NEED TO BE BASHFUL. WE ARE, AFTER ALL, AMONG FRIENDS.
YOU SUCKLE AT THE TIT OF THE NEEDY... THE FAITHFUL...THE HOPEFUL...AND DRAIN EACH AND EVERY ONE OF ALL THAT THEY HAVE AND ALL THAT THEY ARE.
IT IS A VALUABLE GIFT.
AND I DO VALUE THAT GIFT, REVEREND.
HOWEVER...
I W-WILL FIND THE S-SISTER, CONSTANT.
IN M-MY TIME, WE ARE JUST B-BEGINNING TO INTERCONNECT... LOCATING HER HAS BEEN MORE D-DIFFICULT THAN ANTICIPATED, AS YOU CAN SEE, B-BUT I HAVE MANY RESOURCES Y-YET TO EXPLOIT.
I WILL FIND HER.

AGUHKUH!
AHEM. AS I WAS SAYING...
HOWEVER, I AM DEEPLY DISSATISFIED WITH YOUR RECENT PERFORMANCE.
IT IS FOR THAT REASON THAT I AM RELIEVING YOU OF YOUR DUTIES. CYGNET HERE, WITH WHOM YOU ARE BECOMING INTIMATELY FAMILIAR, WILL BE TASKED WITH FINISHING THE JOB THAT YOU STARTED.
AS YOU CAN SEE, SHE HAS A MUCH DIFFERENT MODUS OPERANDI. WHILE YOU WARP THE MINDS OF MEN, PROFESSING FAITH IN A GOD THAT DOES NOT EXIST, SHE GOES DIRECTLY FOR THE HEART.
ONE...TICK-TOCK. TWO...TICK-TOCK. HOW SLOW CAN A MAN'S HEART BEAT BEFORE THE TIDAL FORCE OF DEATH CLAIMS HIS FLESH?
WELL, WE SHAN'T FIND OUT TODAY.
BUT YESTERDAY...
...YESTERDAY, CYGNET WILL FIND THE SISTER.
AND THEN SHE WILL DESTROY HER.

AS THE CONTINUUM COMMANDS.
I SERVE.

San Francisco. 2015.
THE FREEDOM OF ADULTHOOD? FORGET IT.
IN THE BLINK OF AN EYE, YOU'RE REVERTED TO YOUR CHILDHOOD SELF, BEING REMINDED TO TAKE OUT THE TRASH (ALREADY DID!) AND BRUSH YOUR TEETH (OF COURSE!).
THERE'S NOTHING MORE DEPRESSING THAN NEEDING TO MOVE BACK IN WITH YOUR PARENTS.
AND DON'T GET ME STARTED ON CURFEWS...
-CANDI SNYDER, 2015.
HEY, DAD! STILL HAVEN'T OPENED THE GATES?
DOESN'T SMELL LIKE IT.
I'M BETTING ON ANOTHER FIVE MINUTES IN THIS MOSH PIT. I THINK WE'LL MAKE IT THROUGH ALIVE.
THROUGH THE GAME? SURE, BUT COMING BACK HOME...DON'T COUNT ON IT.
MOM'S IN A MOOD.

OH, BOY.
MOOD AS IN, "HE'D BETTER NOT GO OUT DRINKING WITH RON AFTER THE GAME" OR, "DON'T YOU THINK OUR DAUGHTER IS A LITTLE OLD TO BE DRESSING UP?"
PROBABLY MORE OF THE LATTER.
LOOK, KIDDO, PARENTS AREN'T ALWAYS GOING TO UNDERSTAND THEIR KIDS. WE CAN'T. YOU GREW UP IN A COMPLETELY DIFFERENT WORLD. JUST KEEP DOING WHAT MAKES YOU HAPPY.
YOUR MOM'LL COME AROUND EVENTUALLY.
AND, HEY, I DIG THE NEW BLADES. LOOKS LIKE YOU COULD KILL A BOAR WITH 'EM.
BUT THANKS, DAD. HAVE FUN AT THE GAME.
PROBABLY BETTER TO STICK WITH FABRICS. I'M NOT SURE HOW I'D FARE AGAINST MURDEROUS SWINE.

YOU WANT A DOG OR ANYTHING?
ARE YOU KIDDING? LAST TIME I ATE ONE OF THOSE DAMNED THINGS I MISSED THE WHOLE NINTH INNING.
I'M TOO OLD TO KEEP EATING THAT CRA--
THWOOOSH
THE HELL JUST HAPPENED?
BOOM
LOOK! LOOK!
YOU SEE HER?
GIANTS

I... I SEE HER...
CRAAAKOOM
GIANTS
KACRACK
JUST GO. GO!

KNOCK-
KNOCK
COME ON
IN, MOM.

I TAKE
IT YOU HAVE
TODAY OFF.

YEAH, THEY'VE CUT
EVERYONE DOWN
TO PART-TIME
HOURS.

RELAX. I
PUT IN A COUPLE OF
APPLICATIONS WHEN
I WAS OUT THIS
MORNING.

I CUT THROUGH
CHINATOWN ON THE WAY
BACK AND FOUND THIS
BIZARRE LITTLE
SHOP.

PRODUCE IN
THE FRONT AND
KIND OF A YARD
SALE IN THE
BACK.

I PICKED UP
THIS PATTERN
AND THOSE
SCISSORS. OLD
AS DIRT, BUT
THEY CUT LIKE A
KNIFE THROUGH
BUTTER.

BUTTON
ME UP, WOULD
YOU?

DON'T
YOU THINK
YOU SHOULD
WATCH YOUR
SPENDING UNTIL
YOU GET A NEW
JOB?

UNGH... THAT'S--
MOM?!
MOM!
CANDI... MY GOD...

IN THE BEGINNING, THE WEAK WERE SLAIN.

THEIR BODIES WERE DISCARDED OUTSIDE THE *STREAM*, FILLING THE CENTURIES WITH BLOOD.

IT WAS AN EFFECTIVE PRACTICE. THE CONTINUUM STOOD TOGETHER AS ONE, STEADFAST ON THE PATH FOR CONQUEST AND CONTROL. IT WAS OUR GOLDEN AGE.

BUT RESOLVE IS NOT EQUAL IN ALL MEN.

ONE BY ONE THEY WAVERED, AND ONE BY ONE THEY JOINED THEIR BRETHREN IN THE BOWELS OF TIME. I KILLED THEM ALL. I DID SO WITH GREAT PLEASURE.

FOR EACH THAT FELL, I SCOURED TIME AND SPACE FOR A SUITABLE REPLACEMENT. YET, EACH GREW LESS SUITABLE THAN THE ONE BEFORE HIM...AND I LEARNED.

IT IS NOT ENOUGH TO SLAY THE WEAK.

THEY MUST BE SUBJUGATED.

THE CONTINUUM IS THE UNITY OF EXPLOITATION.

- THE CONSTANT.

CIRCA 2617.
CIRCA 1301.
CIRCA 234 B.C.

WHAT IS IT YOU SEE WHEN YOU LOOK INTO THE MIRROR, REVEREND?

WHAT IS YOUR PLACE IN THIS LIMITED UNIVERSE?

MY PLACE...IS IN SERVICE TO THE CONTINUUM, OF COURSE.

YET YOU HESITATE IN WORD AND DEED. YOU, THE FALSE IDOL TO WHOM THE MASSES TURN, HAVE YOU GROWN BORED OF THE POWER THE CONTINUUM PROVIDES?

I THOUGHT NOT.

WHAT WE GIVETH WE CAN TAKETH AWAY, REVEREND.

NO MAN IS SO GREAT THAT WE CANNOT DESTROY HIM.

YOU HAVE SOMETHING TO SAY TO ME, REVEREND? A DISPLEASURE TO VOICE?
BETTER EQUIPPED AND MORE DRIVEN, BUT THAT IS NEITHER THEN NOR NOW.
THERE ARE... NO WORDS THAT WOULD REDEEM ME.
I CAN ONLY HOPE THAT YOUR CYGNET IS BETTER EQUIPPED TO FIND THE SISTER THAN I.
IF I MAY BE SO BOLD AS TO ASK, IF SHE WAS BETTER SUITED FOR HUNTING THE SISTER OF MY TIME...
SIGH. I HAD HOPED THAT WITH YOUR FINESSE WE COULD AVOID SOME RIPPLES, BUT THAT IS NOT TO BE. AND THAT IS WHY YOU ARE STILL HERE, REVEREND.
...THEN WHY WASN'T SHE DEPLOYED SOONER?
I'M BEING TASKED...WITH CLEAN-UP?
WITHOUT MY AEON I CAN'T EVEN RETURN TO MY OWN TIME. HOW DO YOU EXPECT ME TO--
TAKE IT. IT WAS INTENDED FOR THE RELIGION COMMITTEE, AFTER ALL.
GOD HAS INDEED SHONE HIS HOLY LIGHT ON YOU THIS DAY.
I DON'T BELIEVE IN GOD.
RECLAIM YOUR PLACE AMONG US, BROTHER.
NOR SHOULD YOU.
NOW DIP THE ASPERGILLUM INTO THE AEON.

YOUR SCENT BETRAYS YOU.
NOT THE SISTER...BUT HE IS OF THE BLOOD...
HER FATHER.
A SIMPLE MATTER TO FOLLOW THE SHORTEST BRANCH BETWEEN LEAVES ON THE FAMILY TREE!
BLAM
KOW
BLAM
TAK
TAK
TAK

Candi's House.
LISTEN, RON, I'M HOME.
GLAD WE MADE IT OUTTA THAT WARZONE WITHOUT THAT SHE-RA WANNABE BUSTING OUR BALLS, PAL. LATER.
GIANTS
CANDI? LAUREN?!
HUN? BABY, WHERE'S CANDI?
HOW MUCH DID YOU TAKE?!
OH, THANK GOD. YOU WOULDN'T BELIEVE... THE GAME...
I JUST NEED TO SLEEP A LITTLE BIT.

KRRRK
GODDAMMIT!
WHU--
YOUR DAUGHTER ISN'T HERE. IT SEEMS THAT WE JUST MISSED HER.
I'M SORRY, BUT YOU WON'T GET TO SAY GOODBYE.
KUH--
I HOPE YOU UNDERSTAND.
THE SISTERS MUST LEARN THAT THERE IS A PRICE FOR FLEEING THE CONTINUUM...
...EVEN FOR THE BLOOD.
GIANTS

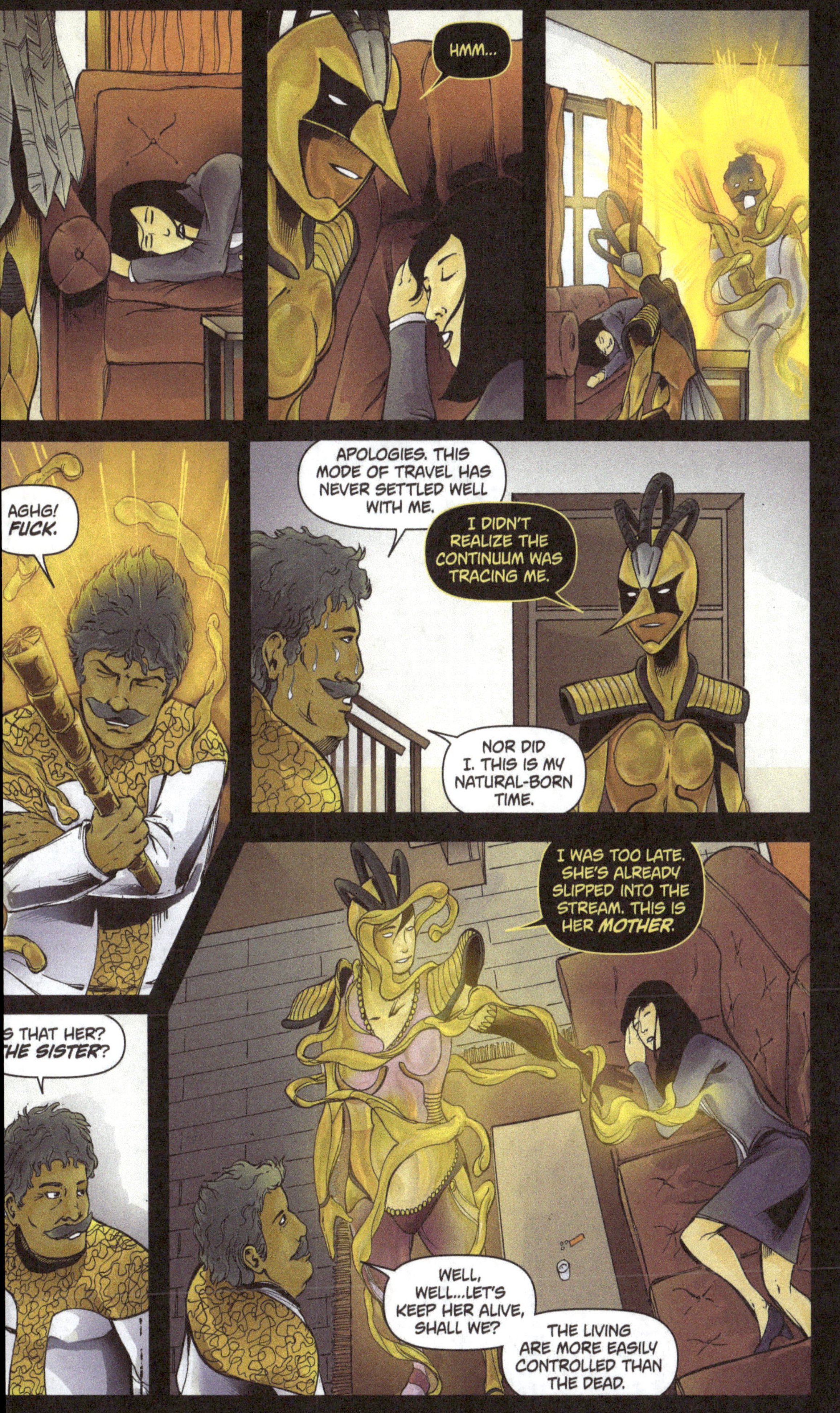

HMM...
AGHG! FUCK.
APOLOGIES. THIS MODE OF TRAVEL HAS NEVER SETTLED WELL WITH ME.
I DIDN'T REALIZE THE CONTINUUM WAS TRACING ME.
NOR DID I. THIS IS MY NATURAL-BORN TIME.
I WAS TOO LATE. SHE'S ALREADY SLIPPED INTO THE STREAM. THIS IS HER MOTHER.
S THAT HER? THE SISTER?
WELL, WELL...LET'S KEEP HER ALIVE, SHALL WE?
THE LIVING ARE MORE EASILY CONTROLLED THAN THE DEAD.

Kai-Fang-Fu, China. 1232.
THE LIVING AND THE DEAD ARE SEPARATED ONLY BY MOMENTS.
GENERAL CUI LI KNOWS THIS ALL TOO WELL. HE HAS BURIED AS MANY BODIES AS HE HAS BURNED.

KTHWWOOOM
BUT HE IS NOT YET WEARY OF WAR.

TO LI, EACH MOMENT IS PRECIOUS.

QUICKLY! THE MONGOL ARE UPON US NOW, FIRE!

THWOOSH
LET THIS END.
≈GASP≈
NO. NO, NO, NO.

WHU--
WHAT THE?!

"WHERE...? WHEN...?
WHEN AM I?"

AT THE END.
IN THE END.

FOREVER WHEN THE
NIGHT RISES, MY GAZE
IS DRAWN TO THE STARS.

WILL I VENTURE THERE ONE DAY, WHEN
MY SOUL PASSES FROM THE FLESH, AND
I STEP INTO THE GREAT BEYOND?

WILL THEY
EMBRACE ME?

-ASHLULTUM.
CIRCA 1590 B.C.

attusa, Capitol of
ittite-Occupied Mesopotamia.
1590 B.C.
MY FINGERS DANCE UPON FABRIC, DRIVEN NOT BY THOUGHT, BUT BY EMOTION.
THE CLOTH UNDER MY FINGERTIPS IS LONELY AND COARSE.
I WILL SHAPE IT AND CRAFT IT INTO SOMETHING WARM.
WITH EACH CUT OF THE SCISSORS THE FABRIC SIGHS IN RELEASE.
IT AWAITS ITS OWN BIRTH.
ASH... LUL...TUM...
-ASHLULTUM, CIRCA 1590 B.C.

YOUR CHAMBERS? THIS IS THE SEWING ROOM.
YOU HAVEN'T MOVED YOUR BED, HAVE YOU?
WOULD YOU BE UPSET IF I DID?
THERE ARE MORE APPROPRIATE WAYS TO ENTER MY CHAMBERS, KATUZILI.
OH, I'M SURE THE LADIES WOULD MISS YOU...

I, HOWEVER, WOULD REACH DEEP WITHIN MYSELF AND FIND THE PERKS TO SUCH AN ARRANGEMENT.
IF I RECALL CORRECTLY, YOU WERE TO TEACH ME HOW TO SEW.
YET HERE I STAND, AS UNSKILLED WITH NEEDLE AND THREAD AS I WAS THE DAY WE MET.
REALLY? AND WHAT WOULD THOSE BE?

I COULD USE THE ONE-ON-ONE ATTENTION.
YET ONLY ONE WHO UNDERSTANDS THE DEPTHS OF MY WIT AND CHARM.
YOU HAVE MANY WIVES WHO'D BE PLEASED TO PROVIDE IT.
COME, LET US FORGET THE LABORS OF THE DAY. THE NIGHT COMES, AND IN THE NIGHT--

--WE DANCE!
PERHAPS YOU SHOULD BE MY CONCUBINE.
I DO MAKE A LOVELY WOMAN.
BUT YOU ARE MOST CERTAINLY NOT A WOMAN...
...AND, SO, ARE NO CONCUBINE OF MINE!
I HAVEN'T TIME FOR MORE PLAY, KATUZILI.
KING KHYANE WILL BE VISITING SOON, AND I HAVE TO HAVE THIS OUTFIT READIED.
THE DESIGN IS LOVELY, ISN'T IT?
I'VE DREAMT OF IT EVERY NIGHT SINCE--
KATU, I--
ASHWAAAAYYYYYT!

Kal-Fang-Fu, China. 1232.
I WILL NOT MOURN FOR YOU, FOOLISH GIRL.
YOU COME TO US AS WE READY OURSELVES FOR THE FINAL CALL.
PREPARE YOURSELF. TODAY, YOU WILL DIE.
RUN, CANDI.
SOMETIMES YOU JUST WANT TO KEEP RUNNING--
TODAY, WE ALL DIE!
WHAT'D...
WHAT'D I DO?

--BUT YOU CAN'T. WHEN THERE'S NOTHING IN THE WORLD THAT MAKES ANY SENSE, THE STRUGGLE ISN'T JUST TO LIVE. I WANT TO LIVE, BUT EVEN MORE...I WANT TO UNDERSTAND.
WHAT'S HAPPENING TO ME?
- CANDI C.1232.
OKAY... HERE WE GO!
UNGH!
THERE ARE MOUNDS OF DEAD ON BOTH SIDES!
ALREADY THE STENCH SUMMONS THE FLIES! HOW SOON UNTIL WE JOIN THEM?

WHAT HAS OUR LOYALTY WROUGHT?!?
I WAS DESTINED TO DIE ALONGSIDE MY MEN THIS DAY, MONGOL.
THAT IS WHERE MY LOYALTY LEAD.
I...I CAN MAKE IT...
BUT IF I LIVE THROUGH THIS DAY, I OWE MY LIFE NOT TO MY MEN, BUT TO A GOBLIN IN ITS GUISE.
SLAM
OH. MY. GOD...

I'M A FUCKING SUPERHERO.
UNBELIEVABLE.
DOWN, GOBLIN!
SLOOOOSH
THUD
I HAVE NEED OF YOUR MAGICS IN THE DAYS TO COME.
PERHAPS YOU COULD STAY WITH ME FOR A TIME.
WELL DONE, GOBLIN.
I OWE YOU A GREAT DEBT.

MY MISSION WITH THE BLUE HATS WILL NOT BE SO FUTILE WITH YOU AT MY SIDE.

Kai-Fang-Fu.
The Pure and Truth
Qing Zhen Si.

WE FACE A CLOUD OF WAR, RATIONED SUPPLIES, AND STARK DAYS,

YET EACH MORNING YOU TEND TO YOUR TASKS WITH BRIGHT SMILES AND WARM SPIRITS.

IT IS MY FAVORITE PART OF THE DAY.

THE COLOR RISES IN HIS CHEEKS WHEN YOU SPEAK, HU JIN. PERHAPS--

YOU ARE IN LOVE, BOHAI SHI... WITH THE FOODS IN OUR CART!

I CAN HEAR YOUR BELLY RUMBLING FROM HERE.

STILL YOUR HEARTS, GIRLS.

WE CANNOT ALLOW FLIRTATION TO DISTRACT OUR YOUNG MEN FROM THEIR DUTIES.

LOVE IS BORN OF PEACE, NOT WAR.

WHERE IS THE LANTERN?
I THINK I LEFT IT ON THE TABLE.

AHHHHHHH!
AIEEEEEE!!!

THE DEMON LILITH!

SHE'S RISEN!

Kai-Fang-Fu, The Clock Tower of Su Song
THEY ARE HERE.
BOTH SISTERS OF THE BLOOD.

Formerly Vancouver, British Columbia. 4490.
AND WE'VE FOUND THEM.
I BRING YOU GLORIOUS TIDINGS, CONSTANT.
WORDS DO NOT BRING GLORY. DEEDS BRING GLORY.
PLEASURE.
PAIN.
THE ACT IS THE NECESSITY. THE WORDS...
THESE WORDS ARE THE REFLECTIONS OF ACTION.
CYGNET HAS TRACKED DOWN THE KNOWN SISTER!
MOREOVER, QUEEN MAKEDA HAS FORWARDED THE TEMPORAL COORDINATES FROM THE SMITH...
...BASED ON THE TEMPORAL GEOMETRY ASSUMED BY CYGNET'S ARMOR.
THIS DESIGN IS KNOWN TO ME.
IT LEADS TO THE TIME OF EMPEROR FREDERIK II.
TELL HIM WHAT YOU'VE TOLD ME.
THE SISTERS ARE IN HIS DOMAIN NOW.
AS YOU COMMAND, MY CONSTANT!
YOU ARE FIRST AMONG MY DESERVED.
YOU WILL GO TO 1232 AND SPEAK WITH FREDERIK ON MY BEHALF.

Kai-Fang-Fu.
The Court of Emperor Aizong.
DO AS YOU ARE ASKED AND YOUR REWARDS WILL BE TEN-FOLD.
STEADY, GOBLIN.
GENERAL CUI LI, MIGHTIEST OF WARRIORS, BESTED BY THE BARBARIAN DREGS CLAMORING AT OUR GATES.
HOW FORTUITOUS THAT YOU--AND YOU ALONE--SURVIVED.

FORTUITOUS INDEED. AS THE MONGOLS SPREAD FORTH, LIKE SPIDERS FLEEING A NEST, YOU WILL NEED YOUR BEST WARRIORS AT YOUR SIDE
YET THE BEST WARRIORS CANNOT BE VICTORIOUS FACED WITH INSURMOUNTABLE ODDS.

THE MONGOL NUMBERS WERE TOO MANY, AND OURS TOO FEW. BUT THE MEN WERE RESOLUTE, MAINTAINING THEIR POSTS IN THE FACE OF CERTAIN DEATH.
THE NORTHERN WALL FELL IN FIRE AND CARNAGE.
EVEN I, WHOSE SKILLS ON THE BATTLEFIELD ARE UNRIVALED, SAW DEATH ON THE HORIZON.

BUT YOU WERE SPARED THIS UNPLEASANT FATE. YOU WERE SAVED.
BY THIS... GOBLIN?
DO NOT LET HER FEEBLE FORM DISSUADE YOU, EMPEROR.

IN A SINGLE DAY SHE HAS DONE MORE FOR OUR CAUSE THAN YOUR BARBARIAN CULT.

THE BLUE HATS ARE WARRIORS OF LEGEND, WHOSE DEEDS AND PROWESS HAVE BEEN WITNESSED FOR GENERATIONS.

THIS CREATURE IS JUST A GIRL.

I SWEAR TO YOU, I HAVE WITNESSED THIS GOBLIN'S MAGIC.
SHE IS NO MERE GIRL.

THE GOBLIN MUST SNARE ALL THREE.
IF ANY STRIKES THE FLOOR OR BREAKS, HER LIFE IS FORFEIT.
THEN I SHOULD LIKE TO SEE THESE POWERS FOR MYSELF.
COOK, BRING ME THREE EGGS.
ON MY COMMAND YOU WILL TOSS THESE EGGS INTO THE AIR, EACH TO A DIFFERENT AREA OF THE COURT.
NO BIG DEAL.
JUST... GOTTA SQUEEZE A LITTLE TIME.
NO PROBLEM.
IS THIS GOBLIN NOT REMARKABLE?
WE SHALL SEE.

WHEW.
C'MON, LITTLE GUY. WE CAN DO THIS.
I KNOW YOU'RE IN THERE.
DO YOU HEAR IT, LI?
THE SOUND OF YOUR SHAME ECHOING THROUGH MY COURT?
TIME TO COME OUT.
AS YOU CAN SEE, EMPEROR, I DIDN'T BREAK YOUR EGGS.
YES, YOU PROVE YOUR MAGICS, GOBLIN...
...BUT THAT WILL NOT FREE YOUR MASTER FROM HIS OTHER OBLIGATIONS.

The Pure and Truth.
Kai-Fang-Fu.
THIS IS WHAT YOU CALL THE DEMON, LILITH?
WE MEAN YOU NO HARM.
TAKE MY HAND, CHILD.
SHE'S JUST A GIRL.
A FOREIGNER, YES, BUT A CHILD OF MEN LIKE THE REST OF US!

NO, GUOTIN SHI. SHE CANNOT BE!
I SAW HER TAKE FORM! WE BOTH DID! SHE FILLED UP, LIMB-BY-LIMB, AS IF A SACK FILLED WITH WATER!
IS THAT WHAT YOU SAW AS WELL, HU?
I...
TELL HIM!
I DO NOT KNOW WHAT I SAW. WE...WE WERE WITHOUT OUR LANTERN...
I UNDERSTAND. IT IS NO WONDER THAT THIS HUNGRY TRAVELER FRIGHTENED AND CONFUSED YOU.
THOUGH SHE MAY LOOK DIFFERENT, WE MUST SET ASIDE OUR FEARS AND EMBRACE THOSE IN NEED.
JUN, I WOULD LIKE YOU TO TAKE THIS YOUNG WOMAN AND PREPARE HER A PROPER MEAL AND BATH.
PROVIDE HER DRESS APPROPRIATE FOR GENERAL CUI LI'S ARRIVAL.
WE ARE BOUNDLESSLY LOYAL TO OUR COUNTRY.
I FEAR OUR NEUTRALITY IN THE CONFLICT BETWEEN OUR JUSEN OCCUPIERS AND WOULD-BE MONGOL CONQUERORS...
...MAY COME TO AN END WITH THE GENERAL'S VISIT.
WE WILL DO WHAT MUST BE DONE.

Lesi, Italy. 1232.

MEN OFTEN SEEK TO REPLACE FAITH WITH EVIDENCE,
BELIEF WITH PROOF.

KING FREDERIK II DREAMS OF THE WORD OF GOD
ON THE TONGUES OF BABES, WHISPERED IN THE
LANGUAGE OF ADAM AND EVE.

HE IS GREETED BY AN INFERNAL SILENCE.

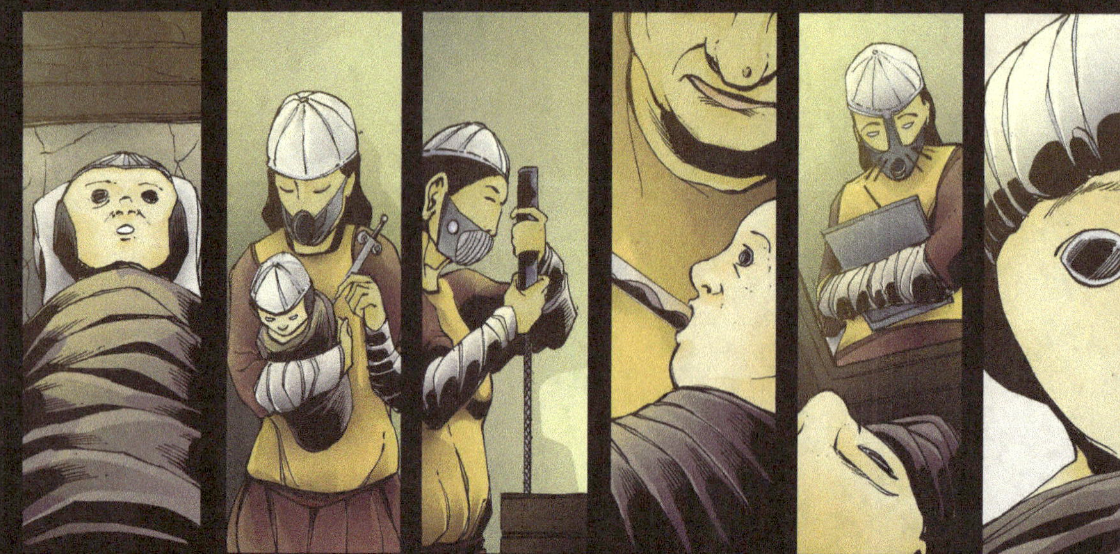

THE CONSTANT TASKS ME WITH ELIMINATING A THREAT TO THE CONTINUUM IN THIS TIME, BUT I HEREBY DELEGATE THIS TASK TO YOU.
CONSIDER IT COMPENSATION FOR MY HOSPITALITY IN YOUR TIME OF EXILE AND AN OPPORTUNITY FOR YOU TO PROVE YOUR WORTH AND REGAIN YOUR PLACE AMONG US.
YOUR HOSPITALITY WILL NOT BE FORGOTTEN, KING FREDERIK.
IT WILL BE MY PLEASURE TO SERVE THE CONTINUUM ONCE MORE.
AND TO LEAVE THIS SENSORY DEPRIVATION SHITHOLE BEHIND.
THERE IS NO BETTER PLACE TO HIDE THAN A HOLY LABORATORY IN WHICH THE STUDIOUS ARE FORBIDDEN BY GOD TO SPEAK.
HERE, THE INNATE LANGUAGE OF THE UNIVERSE WILL MANIFEST SPONTANEOUSLY IN THE TABULA RASA THAT IS THE NEWBORN.
HERE, WE WILL RECEIVE THE LANGUAGE OF GOD.

"I WOULD SAY YOU ARE FORTUNATE, INDEED... SIGNORA PRESIDENT."

San Francisco.
The Present.
--BEFORE THIRD GRADE. HE WAS A WIRY KID WITH A BAD HAIRCUT.
HEH. MY MOM PUSHED ME OUT THE DOOR, THREATENING A FULL ON A--, UH, SPANKING IF I DIDN'T INTRODUCE MYSELF TO THE NEW NEIGHBORS.
I DRAGGED MY FEET ALL THE WAY ACROSS THE LAWN. I DIDN'T WANT TO MEET THIS NEW KID.
I DIDN'T WANT TO BE STUCK HANGING OUT WITH SOME NERD FOR THE REST OF THE SUMMER.
LOU WAS DIGGING AROUND IN A BOX ON HIS FRONT PORCH WHEN HE LOOKED UP AT ME.
HIS FIRST WORDS WEREN'T A HELLO OR EVEN ASKING MY NAME. HE SAID, "YOU PLAY?"
I GLANCED DOWN AT THE BOX, AND SAW A STACK OF CARDS AND A RAGGEDY GLOVE.
THAT'S WHEN I KNEW HE WAS ALL RIGHT...
...BEEN TO A LOT OF GAMES SINCE...
...SOME WITH GIRLS WE NEVER SAW AGAIN.
LATER, WITH OUR WIVES.
AND I'LL NEVER FORGET SNEAKING OFF WITH CANDI, BARELY TWO MONTHS OLD, TO HER FIRST--
LET'S NOT SPEAK OF THE CHILD WHO ISN'T EVEN IN ATTENDANCE AT THIS PAINFUL MEMORIAL.

SHE LOVED YOU, LOU.

I'LL TAKE CARE OF HER.

THERE ARE PEOPLE WHO COME INTO THIS WORLD, BLESSED BY ALL WHO THEY MEET, BUT WHO NEVER LEARN THE VALUE OF THEIR OWN LIFE AND RELATIONSHIPS.

THESE PEOPLE TURN THEIR BACKS ON GOD AND SEEK THEIR SALVATION IN THE PLEASURES OF THIS WORLD.

...SHE BECAME A SELFISH CREATURE, FOCUSED ON HERSELF.

SHE HID HERSELF AWAY IN A SMALL ROOM, DETACHED FROM THE REAL WORLD, COVERING HERSELF IN LAYERS OF DARKNESS.

HER MOTHER AND FATHER WERE WITNESS TO HER DECLINE. HER COMMUNITY THRIVED IN THE CORNERS OF THE COMPUTERS, WHERE DARKNESS AND DEPRAVITY ARE EMBRACED.

LOU GAVE HIS DAUGHTER HIS ALL, BUT HE COULD NOT SAVE HER FROM THE DAMNATION OF HER SOUL...

THERE COULD NEVER BE A MORE PAINFUL THING FOR PARENTS TO WITNESS.

SHE IS THE REASON THAT HER FATHER'S HEART FAILED HIM.

SHE IS THE REASON HER MOTHER TURNED TO ME FOR GUIDANCE.

AND TO ALL OF YOU I SAY, LET US CELEBRATE THE LIFE OF THIS GENTLE MAN, AND CAST ASIDE THE DEMONS THAT HE LEFT BEHIND.

FOR IN HEAVEN, HIS SOUL IS SAFE FROM THE PAINS OF EARTHLY FAILURES, BUT THOSE OF US STILL HERE MUST CONTINUE TO FIGHT AGAINST SIN WITH EVERY BREATH.

CAN YOU BELIEVE THIS CRAP?

BULLSHIT.
BULLSHIT!
THERE ARE THOSE HERE WHO WOULD TURN AWAY FROM THE GLORY OF GOD...
...THOSE MEN, I SAY TO YOU, ARE COWARDS. THEY FEAR GOD'S GAZE. THEY FEAR THE DEPTHS OF THEIR DEPRAVITY AND SIN.
THEY SHOULD.
AND THEY SHOULD.
Candi
BZZZT
Cand
Where are you???

Kai-Fang-Fu, China. The Pure and Truth. 1232.

THERE ARE FEW AMONG THE BLUE HATS WHOSE CHARM AND WIT ARE A MATCH FOR ME.
FEWER STILL WITH A HANDSOME SMILE AND WARM EYES.
TRAITS, I SHOULD SAY, THAT ARE REQUISITE FOR MY FULL ATTENTION!
I WILL PRAY THAT YOU--AND YOUR SISTER--ARE BLESSED WITH THE HEARTS OF THE FINEST MEN.
I, HOWEVER, HAVE NO INTEREST IN SUCH COMPETITION.
IT IS NOT...IN MY NATURE.

THEN WHY WOULD YOU COME TO THE PLACE THAT CONTAINS THE FINEST MEN IN THE LAND?
YOU ASSUME I CAME HERE BY CHOICE.
ENOUGH! WE NEED TO GET READY.
ENOUGH? ENOUGH! SINCE WHEN DO YOU NOT CARE ABOUT THE MEN HERE?
SINCE WHEN? YOU'RE JUST BITTER THAT YOU LOOKED LIKE A FOOL IN FRONT OF THEM.
I AM NOT! THAT WOMAN...
WE HAVE MORE IMPORTANT THINGS THAT NEED OUR ATTENTION.

Kai-Fang-Fu.
THE HUI-HUI MAY OFFER YOU RICHES, GOBLIN, BUT THEY ARE NOT AN HONORABLE PEOPLE.
THEY ARE NOT BOUND BY THE PROMISE OF THEIR WORDS. BE WARY.
THE TREACHEROUS NATURE OF THE BLUE HATS IS WELL KNOWN.
PERHAPS THEY'VE ALREADY TAKEN COUNSEL WITH THE MONGOLS...
IF THAT IS TRUE, EMPEROR AIZONG'S VERY LIFE IS IN PERIL.
ONE SUCH AS YOURSELF, WITH THE POWER OF THE CLOCK, CAN DO MUCH TO SOLIDIFY OUR POSITION.

YOU WILL INTERVENE AS I REQUIRE.

SHOULD THE BLUE HATS REVEAL THEMSELVES, YOU WILL GRASP THE HANDS OF SU SONG'S CLOCK AND STAY THEIR WEAPONS.

I WILL SLAUGHTER THEM AS THE DOGS THAT THEY ARE.

I... OKAY...

IF I CAN'T? OR DON'T? THEN I DIE...

IF I COULD TWIST TIME LIKE HE WANTS, THEN WHY CAN'T I JUST GO HOME?

THE BLOOD FLOWS IN THE STREETS BELOW. AND I FOLLOW IN ITS CURRENT.

The Pure and Truth.
TOO OFTEN, YOUNG
LADIES MISTAKE ARRIVAL
FOR PUNCTUALITY!
OH...UH,
HELLO!
I, UH, AM
PLEASED TO
ANNOUNCE
THE, UM--

--THE LONE DEFENDER OF THE NORTH WALL...
HER GARB...
QUIET!
...MASTER OF GOBLINS, TAKER OF JUSEN CITY--
...GENERAL CUI LI...
GOUTIN, I OFFER MY APPRECIATION FOR THE...EXTRAVAGANT... WELCOME ON THIS DAY.
VERY IMPRESSIVE, TRULY.
I HAVE COME TO OFFER TERMS OF PEACE AND A TREATY, AS WE ARE BOTH FACED WITH THE THREAT OF A CONTINUED MONGOL INCURSION.
INDEED, I CAN SMELL THE STENCH OF THEIR WARRIORS IN THE AIR. EMPEROR AIZONG WILL SEND HIS ARMIES AGAINST THESE DOG-MEN...
...AND THEIR ALLIES.

DAMMIT.
PEEP
THE BLUE HATS HAVE A REPUTATION FOR... GREAT...COMBAT PROWESS. SHOULD--
ABOUT THE CHICK, I MEAN. I'M NEW. TO THE HERALD THING.
UH, HI. SORRY.
THIS IS ALL NEW.
YOU ARE NOT FROM THESE LANDS.

YOU DON'T REALLY LOOK LIKE YOU ARE EITHER.

INDEED, I AM NOT.

HEY, I--

YOUR ATTIRE...I KNOW THE DESIGN.
YOU...WAIT, WHAT?!

HUSH NOW, THERE ARE THOSE WHO STRONGLY FEAR THAT WHICH THEY DO NOT UNDERSTAND.

THERE IS A DANGER TO SAYING TOO MUCH.
THEN WE TALK IN PRIVATE.

WHEN YOU RETURN THIS LITTLE GUY TO ME, ALL RIGHT?

YES, I WILL--

DEATH IS HERE!
AND YOU WILL...
ALL. DIE
THE BLOOD HAS CONVERGED TO THIS PLACE, THIS TIME...
GOBLIN, COME!
THE MONGOLS ARE UPON US ONCE MORE.
HOLD THIS HOLY GROUND!
TO BE CONTINUED...

YOUR ART...
...IT IS AS STILL LIFE IN THE RAPIDS OF TIME.
UMMPF!
IT ENCHANTS WITH SPEED! YOU THINK YOURSELF FASTER THAN A GOBLIN, MONGOL?
YOU CONFUSE SPEED WITH VELOCITY.
I KNOW HER.

I GIFT THIS JAVELIN WITH RATION OF TIME...
...AND LINE OF FLIGHT.
I KNOW YOU! YOU WERE AT THE BALLPARK!
HE IS OF CONSEQUE... HE IS NOT BLOOD...

VELOCITY, YOU SEE.
YOU WERE WITH MY DAD!

WHERE IS HE?!
YOUR WORDS AND ACTIONS ARE CHILDISH AND UNREFINED... ...A TODDLER VYING FOR CONTROL.
YOU BELITTLE THE POWERS AT YOUR DISPOSAL.
THE POWERS AT MY DISPOSAL.
THE NATURE OF THE STREAM, TO SPEED UP, TO SLOW DOWN, TO JUMP, TO POUR, TO STOP.
YOUR FATHER DIDN'T UNDERSTAND, BUT HE DOES NOW. YOU WILL UNDERSTAND...
UNGH!

...AND YOU WILL COME WITH ME.
WHAT ARE YOU--
NO!
SQUEEZE TIME! GOTTA SQUEEZE TIME!!!
SHE HAS TO BE LYING!
SHE DIDN'T KILL HIM!
SHE HAS TO BE LYING!
I WANT... NEED TO KNOW WHAT...WHAT'S HAPPENING.
MEET ME... TOMORROW...AT THE CLOCK TOWER. THEN, WE'LL TALK. REALLY TALK.

The Cretaceous Period.
CONSTANT, EVER A CREATURE PRONE TO COLORFUL ENTRY.
IS IT, PRAY TELL, A RUSE OR DISTRACTION AIMED AT OBSCURING YOUR LATE ARRIVAL?
YOU ARE THE GREAT FABRICATOR, TWAIN.
THE FICTION OF YOUR MIND'S EYE TELLS A GREATER TALE THAN THE CONTINUUM'S TRUTHS.
RAAWWRR!

DICTATE HISTORY AS YOU WILL.
YOUR DISTORTIONS MAY BE LESS CLEVER THAN MINE, OLD FRIEND, BUT THEY ARE FAR LESS PLIABLE.
THE CONTINUUM DOES AS IT PLEASES. FOR MY PART, I HAVE--
I WAS UNAWARE THAT THERE WOULD BE OTHER PARTICIPANTS IN THIS VENTURE.
HAD I KNOWN, I'D HAVE CHOSEN MORE COMFORTABLE ACCOMMODATIONS.
THOUGH IT WOULD APPEAR THAT THIS INTERRUPTION WAS UNANTICIPATED BY YOU AS WELL.
AH, I BELIEVE THAT IS ONE OF YOURS, CONSTANT.
SILENCE, CLEMENS.
NOW, DESERVED, TELL ME WHY YOU DARE INTERRUPT MY PRIVATE EXCURSION.
SPEAK QUICKLY, LEST THE WEIGHT OF YOUR FLACCID FLESH PULL YOUR SPINE FROM YOUR SKULL.
W-WE, WE HAVE, WE HAVE LOST THE CHOSEN. WE HAVE LOST THE CYGNET IN TIME.

WHEN, WASTE?

1232. SHE WAS LOST IN 1232!

FREDERIK, SICKENED BY INSANITY AND FAITH.

GOODFELLOW, RULED BY SHORT-SIGHTED GREED.

SO FEW OF US REMAIN WITH TRUE VISION.

I WILL RETURN TO YOU, CLEMENS. SOON.

OUR ALLIES IN THE CONTINUUM CONTINUE TO DISAPPOINT ME.

THEN, PERHAPS, WE SHALL SEE WHERE YOUR VISION LEADS.

Outside Kai-Fang-Fu. 1232.

<KAI-FANG-FU FALLS TONIGHT, BROTHERS.>*

*TRANSLATED FROM MONGOLIAN.

"THE SKY HERSELF DELIVERS FIRE ON THAT HAVEN OF MONGRELS!"

HAAAIIGH!

STAND, TRAVELER, AND FACE ME.

Hattusa, Capitol of Hittite-Occupied Mesopotamia. 1590 B.C.
YOU BOW NOW BEFORE KATUZILI, FIRST HEIR TO THIS NOBLE PLACE OF YOUR INVASION.
I SAW YOU LEAP FROM THAT PLACE IN THE WIND, THAT SAME PLACE THAT TOOK MY INTENDED.
YOU WITNESSED ANOTHER DISAPPEAR INTO THE WIND THAT BROUGHT ME HERE?
HUH?
WHO?
ASHLULTUM, MY ELUSIVE BETROTHED, FASTENED A CLASP ON A RECEIVING GARMENT SHE TAILORED--
AND THE FABRICS THEMSELVES PLUCKED HER INTO THE SHINING AIR?
YES...

WE CAN FIND HER, KATUZILI. I WANT TO FIND HER.
WILL YOU HELP ME?
YES, IF YOU CAN HELP ME.
MY METAL NEEDS REPAIR, THAT I MIGHT SURVIVE THE STREAM WHERE WAITS YOUR LOVE.
I KNOW OF YOUR TIME, KATU, SO I KNOW I MUST TRAVEL TO EGYPT TO MEND MY PLATE.
EGYPT?
HER KING ARRIVES TO HATTUSA IN A DAY'S TIME.
KHYANE? HERE?
MY FATHER RECEIVES HIM AT CEREMONY TOMORROW!
WHAT FORTUNE! I AM CYGNET, KATU.
WE MUST PROCURE PRECIOUS SALVE FROM THE GOODLY KING KHYANE, AND, THEN...
...THEN, WE GO TOGETHER TO RETRIEVE OUR ASHLULTUM.

Kai-Fang-Fu. The Court of Emperor Aizong. 1232.
YOUR DEVOTION TO THE THRONE IS GREATER THAN I SUSPECTED, GENERAL.
MY COMMENDATION FOR NEGOTIATING THE ASSIGNMENT OF THE HUI-HUI WARRIORS AS MY PERSONAL GUARD.
THEIR SKILLS, THEIR... HERETICAL SENSES... WILL PROTECT ME FROM COMING TREACHERY DURING OUR SUMMIT WITH THE MONGOL LORD.
NEITHER SKILL NOR GOD-GIVEN SENSE SAVED THEIR BROTHERS FROM THE MONGOL BEAST THAT RAVAGED THEIR OWN TEMPLE...
...ONLY THE INTERVENTION OF MY GOBLIN SQUIRE BANISHED THE THING TO THE HELL THAT SPAWNED HER...
...AND SPARED YOUR BLUE HATS AN IGNOMINIOUS SLAUGHTER.

BUT, YES, MY EMPEROR, I CERTAIN GUOTIN'S TROUPE WILL SAVE YOU FROM THE SHARP WORDS OF THE COMING MONGOL ENVOY.
I APPLAUD YOUR PRIDE IN YOUR NEWFOUND CONCUBINE...
...BUT I UNDERSTAND THE ATTACK OF THIS BIRD-WOMAN OF THE MONGOLS WAS THE TURNING POINT IN GUOTIN SHI'S JUDGMENT TO LEND THE BLUE HATS TO MY COURT.
A BRILLIANT DIPLOMATIC PLOY, GENERAL, DESPITE YOUR...RETICENCE.
AS THEY SHOULD.
YOUR COMPLIMENTS STEADY MY IRON RESOLVE, EMPEROR.
NOW, OPEN MY COURT AND ADMIT MY NEW GUARD, AND I WILL BRIEF THEM ON THEIR CHARGE.
THE MONGOL DELEGATION ARRIVES TOMORROW!
COME, GOBLIN. WE TRUST THE EMPEROR TO THE CARE OF OTHERS MORE CERTAIN TO ENSURE HIS FATE.
BEYOND THESE DOORS WAIT THOSE IMPERIAL CHOSEN.

LET US WELCOME THEM TO THE FIRST AND LAST DAYS OF THEIR ROYAL DESTINY.
I KNOW YOU'RE HERE SOMEWHERE...
GENERAL, WE ARE THANKFUL FOR THE ARTS OF YOUR GOBLIN UPON THE ATTACK OF THE MONGOL RAPTOR ON THE PURE AND TRUTH.
WE HOST A DEMON OF OUR OWN WHO WOULD LEARN OF ALL HER TALENTS.
HOW DO YOU--
GOBLIN, COMPORT YOURSELF!

I DON'T KNOW WHERE, OR WHEN, I AM OR HOW I GOT TO THIS PLACE OR AMONG THESE PEOPLE.
I DON'T KNOW WHAT HAPPENED TO MY DAD.
BUT SOME IN THIS PLACE, THIS TIME, SEEM TO KNOW ALL THESE THINGS.
EVEN THINGS ABOUT ME I NEVER KNEW ABOUT MYSELF.
SO, THE ONE THING I DO KNOW...

...IS THAT THIS IS WHERE AND WHEN I BELONG RIGHT NOW.
-CANDI XXXXXXX
C.1232.

KNOCK KNOCK
I'M BUSY, MY FRIENDS, HURRYING TO FIN--
RAFFEPAR ASARFVAN, ASHLULTUM.
YOU... I DON'T UNDERSTAND... WITHOUT MY VEIL...
RIEPAF, ASHLULTUM.
RIEPAF?
RIEPAF.
KNOCK KNOCK KNOCK
ASHLULTUM!

YOU'LL MAKE US LATE, DEMON!
OH! WE... INTERRUPTED YOU!
IS THERE NO END TO THE WAYS BY WHICH YOU DISRESPECT THIS HOUSE, LILITH?
NO! I... WAS ALMOST... FINISHED...
SO WE SEE.
WE LEAVE YOU TO COMPLETE YOUR TASK, FRIEND!
FIND US AT THE MARKET ONCE YOU...GATHER YOURSELF.
WE HAVE MUCH TO PREPARE BEFORE THE MONGOL ARRIVES!
BUT, FOR ME, A MORE PRESSING NEGOTIATION AWAITS.

Kai-Fang-Fu.

WHERE IS THIS GIRL WITH NOTHING TO TRADE?
YOU HAVE NOTHING TO TRADE, GIRL! MOVE ON!

NOTHING IS WHAT I SEE ALL DAY! NOTHING HAS VALUE TO ME!
BRING ME YOUR NOTHING, GIRL...

...AND TAKE A CHICKEN IN EXCHANGE.
I BRING... NOTHING... TO GIVE YOU, SIR.
THEN, I HAPPILY ACCEPT YOUR DEAL AND--

SHWAAAK
WAAAGH!

THAT ONE WAS A FAVOR.
THE ONES WITH DEAD SENSES HOLD BACK YOUR WHOLE SOCIETY, ESPECIALLY DURING WAR.
THE NEXT ONE IS FOR FUN.
SISTER, RUN! THAT MONGOL MONSTER--
WAIT, HU. IT SPEAKS...

JUST THREATS TO DISTRACT US!
SHWAAAK
LISTEN!
YOU'LL ALL BURN, EVERY ONE! UNTIL SOMEONE TELLS ME...
WHERE ARE THE WOMEN FROM OUT-OF-TIME?
THEY DON'T LOOK LIKE YOU!
SHWAAAK
JUN, LET'S GO!
THAT CHILD...
DON'T BE AFRAID.
THEY WIELD TIME MAGICKS FOR IMPOSSIBLE FEATS!
THRUUM

WHO HAS SEEN--
YOUR PARDON, DEMONESS!
I KNOW WHERE THESE CREATURES ARE AND WHEN THEY WILL BE TOGETHER.
I CAN GIVE THEM TO YOU!
DEMONESS? NOT A TYPICAL HONORIFIC FOR A HEAD OF STATE.
TRY MADAME PRESIDENT.
THAT'S IT EXACTLY. NOW, CONVINCE THIS EXECUTIVE POWER YOU WEREN'T BLUFFING TO SAVE YOUR PEOPLE.
ONE IS IN OUR HOME.
SO, THE SISTERS ARE HERE.
WE GO TO THEM NOW.
MADAME... PRESIDENT?
A DEMON ARRIVED FROM NOWHERE, FROM DARKNESS ITSELF!
THE OTHER IS IN THE EMPEROR'S COURT, A GOBLIN THAT MOVES WITHOUT BEING SEEN.
JUN!

I HAVE SOMETHING OF YOURS.
I THINK HE MISSED YOU.
PEEP

THANKS! I, UH, MISSED HIM, TOO. OUR COSTUMES... YOU WEREN'T KIDDING.
NO, WE ARE BOUND IN SOME WAY, MY FRIEND.
CALL ME CANDI.
ASHLULTUM, CANDI.
ASH-WHAT-NOW?
ASHLULTUM. IT IS MY NAME.
HOW DID YOU COME HERE, TO KAI-FANG-FU, ASHLUH...UH... ASH?
I WAS FITTING THE CROWN OF THIS COSTUME...
AND THE FABRIC CAME TO LIFE AND SQUEEZED YOU INTO LITTLE BITS THAT FLEW THROUGH SOME GOLDEN PORTAL, THEN PILED UP TO FORM A NEW YOU HERE, RIGHT?
...AND FASTENED ITS CLASP--
SOMETHING LIKE THAT, YES.

BUT WHY?

WHAT ABOUT THESE OUTFITS WOULD BRING ME HERE TO THIS PLACE, THIS TIME, WITH YOU?

I CAME FROM ANOTHER PLACE AND TIME, TOO, CANDI.

SOMETHING DREW US HERE TOGETHER, BUT I HAVE ONLY ONE CLUE WHAT THAT MIGHT BE.

MY SCISSORS!

I DID NOT BRING THIS WITH ME WHEN I CAME HERE.

I USED THESE SHEARS TO CRAFT MY GARB.

YOUR SCISSORS FOLLOWED AFTER ME.

THEY MAKE MAGICAL CLOTHES!

YES, CLOTHES THAT ARE MAGICAL, LIKE THOSE OF A SORCERER.

WE BOTH USED THE SCISSORS. WE BOTH ENDED UP HERE.

YOU SAW WHAT I CAN DO IN THIS COSTUME, THE POWERS I HAVE!

YOU HAVE THOSE POWERS, TOO, ASH! IT JUST MAKES SENSE!

PERHAPS YOU CAN SHOW ME HOW, THEN.

OKAY, SEE THAT NEXT BUILDING OVER?
WE'RE GOING TO RUN TO IT.
AND HOW DO YOU TRAVERSE THE AIR BETWEEN?
BY SQUEEZING TIME.
WE SHRINK THE TIME IT TAKES TO GO THE DISTANCE, AND OUR VELOCITY GOES WAY UP.
WE GO FASTER?
FASTER!
GO.
WE.
YOU DID IT, ASH!
WE GOTTA FIGURE HOW TO USE THESE COSTUMES, THESE SCISSORS TO GET BACK WHERE WE CAME FROM--
YOU...YOU REALLY MEAN THAT, DON'T YOU?
YES, WE DID!
THAT'S JUST ONE TRICK.
TO FIND WHAT HAPPENED TO YOUR FATHER.
I REALLY DO.

En route to Kai-Fang-Fu.

NOW IS THE TIME TO END THIS LOSS OF LIFE.

WHILE KAI-FANG-FU REMAINS YET UNCONQUERED, HER FALL TO KHAN OGEDAI IS SIMPLY A MATTER OF TIME.

CERTAINLY, EMPEROR AIZONG MUST SEE THIS AND AGREE TO THE TERMS OF HIS MONGOL BETTERS, SO TO PREVENT THE DEATHS OF HIMSELF, HIS THINNING TROOPS, AND THE VERY POPULACE OF HIS FINE CITY.

OF COURSE, THERE ARE SUPERSTITIOUS WHISPERS AMONG OUR RANKS OF GOBLIN SOLDIERS FIGHTING FOR AIZONG'S JOSEN ARMY.
OF AIRBORNE DEMONS SURVEILLING OUR MOVEMENTS AND TACTICS.
ALL JUST THE RAMBLINGS OF DESPERATE MEN IN HARM'S WAY, I ASSURE YOU, AND NOT REAL ASSETS TO BE LEVERAGED BY EMPEROR AIZONG.
IN FACT, HE HAS NO LEVERAGE AT ALL.
AND THAT IS WHY WE SO APPRECIATE YOUR INFLUENCE AND YOUR KIND OFFER OF MEDIATION!
HIS SUPPLY LINES ARE BLOCKADED. HIS TROOPS ARE DEAD OR DEFECTING. HIS PEOPLE ARE STARVING.
BUT, NONETHELESS, WE DO EXPECT AIZONG TO RESIST OUR KHAN'S PEACEFUL OVERTURES, TO PROLONG THE SUFFERING OF HIS PEOPLE IN THE NAME OF NAUGHT BUT PRIDE.

HOLY ROMAN EMPEROR FREDERIK II, PLEASE ACCEPT THE THANKS OF KHAN OGEDEI HIMSELF, TO BOTH YOU AND YOUR INTERPRETER DURING YOUR VOW OF SILENCE.
HIS ROYAL HOLINESS SPEAKS THROUGH ME IN THE SPONTANEOUS TONGUE OF GOD, AMBASSADOR ENKHTUYA.
HIS EXPERIMENTS WERE A SUCCESS!
AND IN THIS IMMACULATE LANGUAGE OF THE UNIVERSE, WE WILL CONVINCE GOOD EMPEROR AIZONG TO CONCEDE KAI-FANG-FU TO THE KHAN, AND WE REQUIRE ONLY ONE REWARD IN RETURN.
WHAT IS YOUR CONDITION?
GOD INFORMS ME THAT THERE TRULY ARE GOBLINS AND DEMONS AMOK IN KAI-FANG-FU.
WHEN I DELIVER THE CITY TO YOU, ALL GOBLINS AND DEMONS ARE FORFEIT TO ME.

San Francisco.
Reverend Goodfellow's
Silver Sanctuary.
2016 A.D.
THRUST INTO THE UNKNOWN.
THAT'S ME NOW.
UNKNOWN TIME.
UNKNOWN PLACE.
MAKE A TRUE OFFERING, BROTHER!
MY BAD, BUT PRINCE ALBERT IS HOLDING ALL MY PRECIOUS METALS.
I'LL PUT YOU TWO IN TOUCH.

IT'S SAID WE ALL FEAR *NOTHING* MORE THAN THE UNKNOWN.
BUT--
WITH THE RIGHT KNIFE...
...I CAN FIT *ALL* OF YOUR PARTS ONTO THAT LITTLE PLATE...
...AND OFFER *YOU* UP TO THE HEAVENS.
BUT NOT ME, NOT ANYMORE.
BLESS YOU, BROTHER.
I SAW MY LIGHT IN THIS TIME. I FOUND MY ANCHOR IN THIS PLACE.
CANDI. 1232 A.D.

GET SKINNY, BREEDERS.
♪♫PHRUM-PHRAH-PHRUMPH♫♪
CLAP CLAP CLAP CLAP CLAP CLAP
IT'S HIGH TIME, MY CHILDREN.
HIGH. TIME!
HIGH TIME WE REVEAL TO EACH OTHER OUR TRUE FACES AND THE EVILS THAT DWELL BENEATH THEM!
THERE YOU ARE. NOW, WHERE'S CANDI?

Kai-Fang-Fu, China.
The Palace of Emperor Aizong.
1232.
THE SENTINEL STANCE BUILDS DISCIPLINE, SHARPENS VIGILANCE, GENERAL.
IN FOUR HOURS, THEY SHIFT TO THE OPPOSITE LEG, AVOID TIRING.
UNARMORED CONTORTIONISTS WILL NOT PREVENT THE TREACHERY OF THE MONGOLS, RABBI.
YOUR SONS WILL BUT SLOW THE PROJECTILES OF THE NORTH WITH THEIR OWN AGILE TISSUES.
DEFENSE OF A THING IS MORE THAN SIMPLY BEING BETWEEN IT AND ITS ASSAILANT!
WHAT IS THIS CEREMONIAL PREENING, GUOTIN?
THERE IS DISTRACTION. REDIREC--
GUOTIN SHI!
HELLO, ASHLULTUM.
HAI!
BOHAI!
YOU WATCH! NO TALK!
HU NEEDS YOUR GUIDANCE ON THE... AH...THE MENU...
WHERE IS SHE?

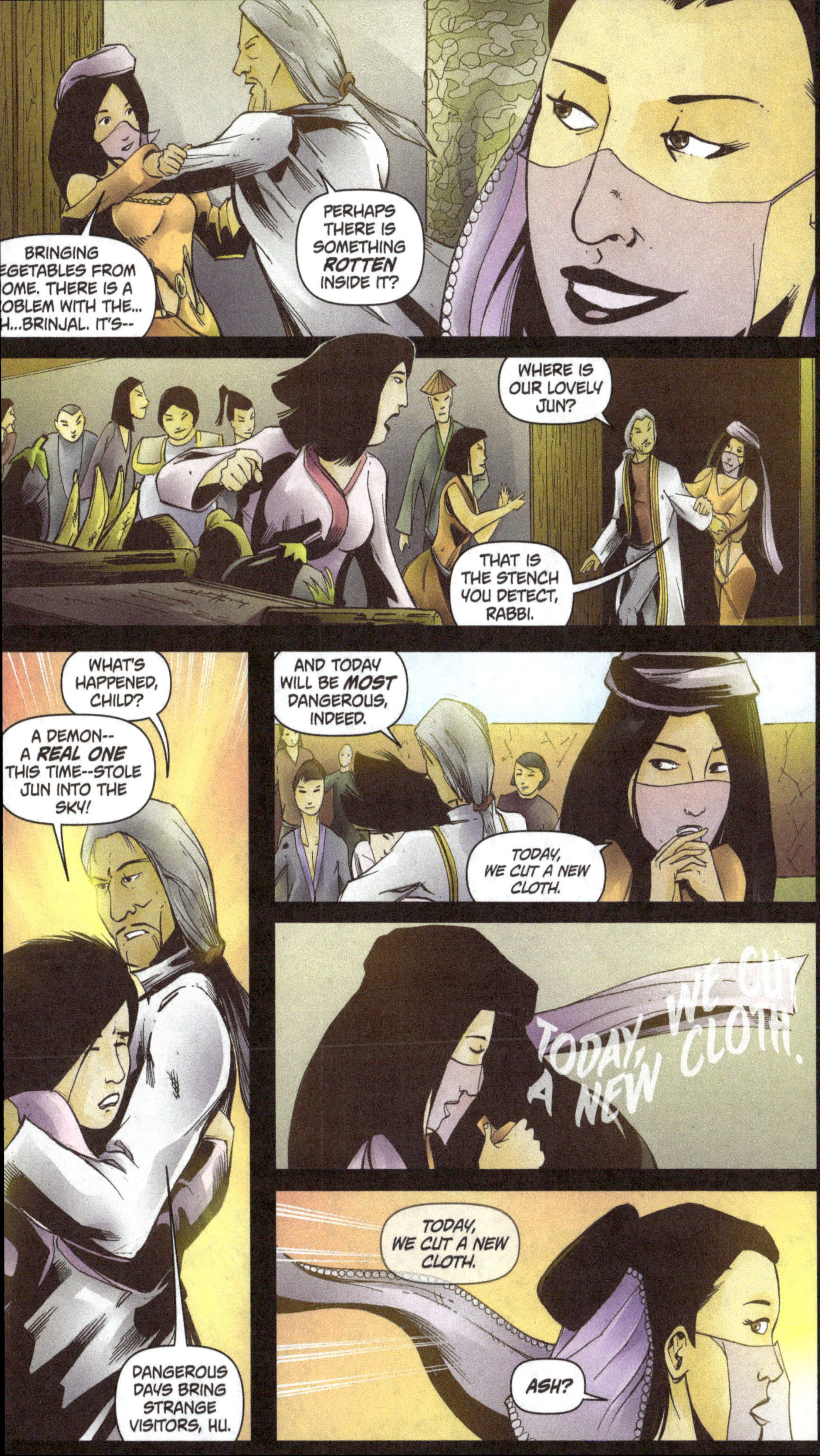

BRINGING VEGETABLES FROM HOME. THERE IS A PROBLEM WITH THE... UH...BRINJAL. IT'S--
PERHAPS THERE IS SOMETHING ROTTEN INSIDE IT?
WHERE IS OUR LOVELY JUN?
THAT IS THE STENCH YOU DETECT, RABBI.
WHAT'S HAPPENED, CHILD?
A DEMON-- A REAL ONE THIS TIME--STOLE JUN INTO THE SKY!
AND TODAY WILL BE MOST DANGEROUS, INDEED.
TODAY, WE CUT A NEW CLOTH.
TODAY, WE CUT A NEW CLOTH.
DANGEROUS DAYS BRING STRANGE VISITORS, HU.
TODAY, WE CUT A NEW CLOTH.
ASH?

Nearby.

NOW THAT WE HAVE ACHIEVED PRIVACY...

BY NOW, THEY... THEY WILL BE AT THE IMPERIAL PALACE FOR THE, UH, RECEPTION...
...FOR THE MONGOL ENVOY...

OH, THESE GIRLS HAVE STATUS ALREADY. THEIR REPUTATION ACROSS THE STREAM IS WELL-EARNED.
YOU WISH TO KILL THEM?

LET'S TALK. THE DEMON AND HER GOBLIN. WHERE ARE THEY NOW?

NOT TODAY.
THEIR LIVES OUTVALUE THEIR DEATHS AT THIS POINT IN THE STREAM.
I GIVE THEM TO YOU.
THIS IS MY EYE. TURN IT ON THESE SISTERS WHEN YOU SEE THEM, AND I WILL SEE THEM.
THEN, I COME FOR THEM.
I KNOW YOU WILL, AND THIS WILL ENSURE I GET THE RIGHT ONES.
BUT THERE WILL BE GUARDS... WARRIORS...
THEM I ORDER EXECUTED TODAY.

I WAS NEVER AFRAID OF THE DARK.
EVEN THE SUBJECT OF BENEFICENT OWNERS, I WAS, NONETHELESS, OWNED.
AND, SO, SAW SIGHTS OF GRIEVING PAIN TO OVERWHELM THE SENSES.
IN THOSE MOMENTS, THE DARK WAS WELCOME.

N THOSE MOMENTS, I HELD THE DARK TO ME AS THE SOFTEST LOVER ON THE COLDEST NIGHT.
ASHLULTUM. 1232 A.D.
THE POSTURING BEGINS WITHOUT PAUSE FOR PLEASANTRIES, GOBLIN.
TAKE HEED. IMAGINE THE END OF A DAY THAT BEGINS AS THIS.
HIS EMINENCE, AMBASSADOR ENKHTUYA, TONGUE OF KHAN OGEDAI!
KAI-FANG-FU WELCOMES YOU, AMBASSADOR.
I BRING TERMS FROM THE KHAN, GENERAL.
AND GUESTS...

HOLY ROMAN EMPEROR FREDERIK II...
...AND HIS CONSTANT COMPANION!
YOU APPEAR MORE CONCUBINE THAN COMBATANT, LITTLE SISTER.
SO, YOU ARE THE GOBLIN SO LEGENDARY ON THE TONGUES OF THESE ARMIES!
STEADY, GOBLIN.
WOULDN'T YOU SAY, EMPEROR?
WHY, YES, EMPEROR, PERHAPS SHE EARNS THE RANK OF GOBLIN FROM THE FILTHY DEPRAVITY OF HER CARNAL ACHIEVEMENTS AMONG THE LEGIONS OF AIZONG.
HOLD, CANDI.
LEGENDARY, INDEED.

KLICK

GOBLIN! WHERE IS LIL--ASHLULTUM?
JUN? WHERE DID YOU--

TAKE ME TO ASHLULTUM. I MUST WARN HER OF THE ONE WHO STOLE ME!
SHE IS IN-INSIDE WITH RABBI GUOTIN...

...TO TASTE THAT ICHOR OF SWEET ARBITRATION.
KLICK
EMPEROR AIZONG, YOUR HIGHNESS!
TODAY WE SUBSTITUTE TONGUES FOR SWORDS...

IT'S DONE. *HAVE* THE OUTLANDER BITCHES AND LEAVE US BE.
NOW, WE BUT SEEK A *DEMON* PAIRED WITH OUR GOBLIN, AND YOU MAY TAKE YOUR LEAVE, YOUR HOLINESS.
HU!
HU, GET *AWAY* FROM HER!
JUN!
JUN?!
LET'S *GO!*
WHAT ARE YOU *DOING?* THIS IS--
AND *THERE* YOU ARE! SO SIMPLE, EVEN *LOBOTOMIZED* REGENTS DIVINE YOU, EH, FREDERIK?
YOU SEEK *ME?*

I SOUGHT YOU ACROSS SEVEN EPOCHS, GIRL, AND HERE YOU STAND, THE BOTH OF YOU STRANDED AT A CONFLUENCE OF STAGGERING FAILURES AND IGNORANT OF YOUR OWN SIGNIFICANCE.
DELIGHTFUL.
EMPEROR AIZONG!
HIS HOLINESS, FREDERIK II, HOLY ROMAN EMPEROR, BIDS YOU WELCOME AND LENDS HIS SEASONED MIND TO THESE HARSH NEGOTIATIONS!
HIS ARE INSIGHTS DELIVERED FROM THE VERY CRANIUM OF GOD!
THE COURT OF AIZONG GRACIOUSLY ACCEPTS THE THOUGHTS OF SO CELEBRATED AN INTELLECT.
SEE FOR YOURSELF.

...BUT HIS HOLINESS TAUGHT ME THE FULL VALUE OF TONGUES IN HIS BRIEF SOJOURN.
LOST OF BRAIN HE MAY NOW BE...
PARTAKE IN MY LABIAL LOQUACIOUSNESS.
RELEASE HER, DAMN YOU!
HEY!
CANDI!
SKREENG
GUHK..
SHWAAAK
≥HNNG!
OH, EVEN MORE CHAOS THAN I FORESAW!

MY THANKS, PRESIDENT EVRA.
I WON'T LET YOU END ME, CONSTANT. THE SISTERS WERE MY TICKET BACK TO THE MOON AND BACK INTO THE CONTINUUM, BUT, GOD DAMN IT, YOU GOT TO THEM FIRST.
I WILL NOT BE UNDONE BY COINCIDENCE IN YOUR HAND!
SHWAAAK
COINCIDENCE? YOU, OF ALL THE CONTINUUM, ARE EXPERT AT INSULT, MADAME PRESIDENT.
ALLOW ME A SKILLED ARBITER ON MY BEHALF TO ARGUE INTENT OVER FELL COINCIDENCE!
BUT OURS IS NOT THE MOST PRESSING GRUDGE AT HAND.
YAAIIIGGGHHH!

FINISH YOUR TASK. KILL THE SISTERS AND RETURN WITH ME TO THE CONTINUUM. NOW.
HUUGHK!
THEY KEEP CALLING US SISTERS!
SHWAAAK
CANDI...
YOU ALREADY DISAPPOINT ME, MADAME PRESIDENT!
AND I REALLY HOPE WE'RE NOT. SISTERS, I MEAN. THIS IS GONNA GET...
MY GUN... YOU TOOK MY GUN!
KILL THEM!
CANDI...

BUT I DON'T NEED MY PIECE IN HAND TO WIELD IT! WELCOME TO THE TWENTY-FOURTH CENTURY, BITCHES!
DIM YOUR HELLFIRES AND FIGHT, WOMAN!
KLIK
...AWKWARD.
...STOP. WE ARE NOT SISTERS, BUT WE WILL SHARE A GRAVESITE...
...IF YOU DO NOT RETURN THIS WEAPON TO ITS OWNER RIGHT NOW!
RETURN IT?
OH, YOU MEAN... TEAMWORK!
LIKE SISTERS.

WHAT ARE YOU DOING, ASH? THIS GUY--
HER GARB! CANDI, SHE'S FROM SOMEWHEN ELSE, LIKE US. HER PATTERN WILL TAKE US FROM HERE!
BITTERSWEET, TO WITNESS MAJESTIC SELF-DISCOVERY MID-PROCESS.
AH, TO END SUCH AN EPIC AS IT BEGINS!
IF I'D NOT KILLED AND RAPED FATE, I'D THINK HER SHINING ON ME THIS DAY.
PERHAPS SHE FORGAVE ME AS I FORGIVE YOU, MADAME PRESIDENT.
ASH, WE GOTTA GO!

WE GO FASTER?
WE GO--

--FASTER!
:SIGH:
FATE'S GRUDGE PERSISTS.
I HAVE NEED OF THAT STEED.
WHERE IS THE AMBASSADOR?
TEDIOUS.
NO MORE QUESTIONS.

LEGS ENOUGH TO MATCH MY QUARRY.
TIME ENOUGH TO ENSNARE THEM IN ITS HOUR-BARE THREADS.

Kai-Fang-Fu, China.
The Palace of Emperor Aizong.
1232 A.D.

MEAGER ARE THE REWARDS FOR SERVING A PEOPLE.

SO ENDS THE SIEGE.

NOW COMES THE INCURSION.

FALL NAMELESS AND UNSEEN AND FORGOTTEN AND DEFENDING THEM STILL.

PROTECT THEM FROM INVADERS, THIEVES, MURDERERS, AND, MOST TIMES, THEMSELVES.

GENERAL CUI LI, DEFENDER OF KAI-FANG-FU, 1232 A.D.

The Streets of Kai-Fang-Fu.
YAH!
MAKE WAY BY ORDER OF EXALTED AIZONG HIMSELF!
WHERE ARE YOU TAKING ME, RABBI?
YOU HAUL THE VERY THRONE OF KAI-FANG-FU IN A CHICKEN CART!
WE RIDE TO SAFETY, MY LORD.
SOMEHOW, THE CITY MUST SURVIVE MOMENTS WITHOUT HER BEATING HEART WHILST WE MUTE ITS RHYTHMS AGAINST STALKING EARS.
INDEED, THE BATTLEFIELD IS UNBECOMING OF AN EMPEROR'S MAJESTY.
WHEN MY GENERAL SECURES THE THEATER, I EMERGE.
WE FLED THE ONSLAUGHT OF THAT BEAST IN THE COURT AT YOUR BEHEST, AND NOW WE HIDE?

SILENCE, BOHAI!
WE DEFEND OUR EMPEROR WITH BOUNDLESS LOYALTY TO OUR COUNTRY, OR DO YOU FORGET ALL I TAUGHT YOU?
APOLOGIES, FATHER.
THE DEVIL WE KNOW LIES SAFE WITHIN MY REACH.
I WILL NOT FORSAKE HIM, DESPITE HIS COWARD--
THEY'RE ALL STUCK IN TIME...
I THINK THEIR CLOCK JUST TICKS SLOWER THAN OURS WHEN I RUN.
SO, THEY'RE STILL MOVING, JUST TOO GRADUALLY FOR US TO NOTICE?

YOU'RE SAVED.
IT'S TRUE!
ASSASSINS!
EXACTLY. GIVES US TIME TO CATCH UP AND SAVE THE EMPEROR!
GOBLIN ASSASSINS EMBEDDED IN MY OWN RANKS!
NO, YOUR HIGHNESS, WE CAME TO SAVE YOU!
THAT MURDEROUS BEASTIE IN YOUR COURT COMES FOR YOU NOW!
THAT WAS THE PLAN OF THE MONGOLS FROM THE START!
MURDER THEIR OWN ENVOY AND CAST CULPABILITY ON MY REGIME.
AND THEN KILL YOU WITH RIGHTEOUS JUSTIFICATION.
BUT IT WAS NOT WE WHO KILLED THE AMBASSADOR.
IT WAS HIS OWN ARCANE ADVISOR!
AND ONLY WE CAN PROTECT YOU, MY LORD.
YEAH, WE GOT SKILLS.

THE SUREST PROTECTION FOR OUR EMPEROR IS ABSENCE FROM THE BATTLEFIELD.
BOHAI, TAKE OUR THREE CHAMPIONS AND FACE THE MONGOL KILLER BESIDE ASHLULTUM AND THE GENERAL'S GOBLIN.
THE REST OF OUR GUARD WILL ESCORT THE EMPEROR INTO OBSCURITY UNTIL THE THREAT IS ENDED.
A STRATEGY WORTHY OF THE THRONE OF KAI-FANG-FU!
DALLY NOT. GO NOW INTO LEGEND!
THIS EVIL CANNOT DEFEAT YOU, BOHAI!
YOUR BLOOD BOILS WITH YOUR FATHER'S SELF-SAME FURY!
WHAT JUST HAPPENED?
WE BECAME THE FINAL LINE OF DEFENSE FOR THIS ASSAULT ON OUR CITY.
WE BECAME BUT MARTYRS FOR ANOTHER COWARD IN A GOLDEN CHAIR.
WE BECAME... ANGSTY.

The Imperial Palace.
THE MONGOL DIPLOMAT LIES DEAD IN THE IMPERIAL PALACE, MEN.
KAI-FANG-FU WILL BE SACKED BY NEXT DAWN, LEST WE FIND OUR EMPEROR AND PRESENT HIM TO NEGOTIATE DIRECTLY WITH THE ENEMY.
DO YOU RIDE WITH ME?
≥GHFF!≤
SCHLL
UNGH!
YOU SPARE ME FOR THE SAKE OF HUMILIATION, MONSTER?!?

I SPARE YOU THAT YOU BE VOYEUR TO MY LUST FOR THE BLOOD OF YOUR CITY, GENERAL.
THESE ARE MY PEOPLE!
THEN, BURY THEM WELL, FOR I WILL NOT BE DENIED THE HOT WET OF THEIR FLESH.

SCARLET PETALS TO PAVE THE CARPET 'TWIXT ME AND MY QUARRY.
THE LEGENDS ARE TR--
--OOH

HE'LL MASSACRE THE ENTIRE CITY, JUN!
JUST STAY DOWN HERE AND LET HIM PASS!
YOUR PRESIDENT... SHE TOOK YOU AND THEN TRIED TO KILL THAT THING OUT THERE.
AND YOU SEE WHAT THAT GOT HER!
ASH-LILITH AND THE GENERAL'S GOBLIN MURDERED HER BEFORE THIS LATEST MONSTER TO TERRORIZE OUR CITY FOR THE SAKE OF STALKING THEM.
WE SURPASS THE POINT OF AN OFFICIAL ESCORT, GENTLEMEN, BUT ACCEPT MY GRATITUDE FOR THE GESTURE.
AND WE MUST GIVE THEM TO HIM, SO THEY CAN DESTROY EACH OTHER AND LEAVE US TO OUR OWN WARS.
STOP! I CAN TAKE YOU TO THE ONES YOU WANT!
THEY GO TO PROTECT THE EMPEROR AT THE PURE AND TRUTH... OUR HOME.
TAKE THEM AND LET OUR CITY FALL TO SIEGE AND NOT SLAUGHTER.
I SEEK NO GUIDANCE IN MY ART, BITCH.
HU, WAIT! OUR LIVES ARE NOTHING TO THESE THINGS!

CARNAGE IS MERE FOREPLAY TO THE CLIMAX OF MY QUEST FOR SATISFACTION THIS DAY.
GLUK...
HU!
SISTERS ARE TRULY MY WEAKNESS, BUT TWINS?
HOW RARE TO PARTAKE OF BOTH SIMULTANEOUSLY!
NO MORE SISTERS DIE TODAY!
YOU STAND CHALLENGED, MURDERER!
BEHOLD, MEN VERSED IN A COMBAT BEYOND YOUR OWN.

PARTAKE OF WARRIORS TRANSCENDENT OF FEAR...
...OF DESPAIR...
...OF DEFEAT!

ARE YOU CERTAIN THIS WILL WORK, CANDI?
ALL WE CAN DO IS TRY TO SEND THIS DUDE BACK TO NARNIA OR WHEREVER HE CAME FROM...
...AND MAYBE HITCH A RIDE RIGHT THE HELL OUT OF HERE, OURSELVES.
AND HOW DO WE MAKE THIS HAPPEN?
WE BOTH AFFECT TIME... SOMEHOW...
ANYWAY, WE DO IT DIFFERENTLY.
I SEEM TO CONTROL HOW TIME AFFECTS THE PROPERTIES OF REAL THINGS, BUT YOU--
--ALTER THE FLOW OF TIME AROUND THINGS.
RIGHT!
I SPIN THE CLOCK AT SUPER-SPEED TO GET TIME MOVING FASTER.
YOU PULL TIME THROUGH IT LIKE WATER OVER A WHEEL, AND I THROW HIM INTO THE CURRENT.
HE GOES BACK WHERE HE CAME FROM, AND, MAYBE, SO DO WE.
OR SOMETHING LIKE THAT...I DUNNO. I TOTALLY FLUNKED PHYSICS IN HIGH SCHOOL.
I TRUST YOU, CANDI.
NO PRESSURE, RIGHT?
THEY'RE HERE. IT'S TIME.
HOLD TIGHT, ASH.
CANDI?

MANZALTU, CANDI.
GOOD STARS?
YEAH... THE BEST STARS...
AMAZING STARS.
NOW, I'M READY.
READY DOESN'T BEGIN TO DESCRIBE IT.

SKREEEK
YOU MOVE BEAUTIFULLY, BOY...
...BUT MY AFFECTIONS ARE MORE AMBITIOUS THIS DAY.

I'M A SUPERHERO.
A FUCKING SUPERHERO!
PREMATURE EJECTION...

...BUT EXHILARATING NONETHELESS.
TIME TO LEAVE.

SOMETIMES, HOME STOPS BEING A PLACE.
AND IT'S WHEN THAT SAFE HARBOR BECOMES A "WHO", MORE SO THAN A "WHERE"...
...IT'S *THEN* WE BECOME MOST LOST NAVIGATING THE PATH BACK THERE.
ASHLULTUM, 2837 A.D.

WHY AM I STILL HERE? I SHOULD'VE GONE--
ON YOUR FEET, GOBLIN.
KAI-FANG-FU IS INDEBTED TO YOU FOR VANQUISHMENT OF THAT GALLOPING DEVIL.
SHE DISPATCHES US NOW TO FULFILL OUR FINAL DUTY IN HER SERVICE.
YOU RECEIVED MY COURIER, RABBI?
YES, GENERAL. OUR LOYALTY REMAINS BOUNDLESS.
BOUNDLESS TO COUNTRY AND BLIND TO THRONE.

THAT MOMENT WHEN YOU'RE BY YOURSELF...
...IN THE ENTIRETY OF THE UNIVERSE...
...WHEN FEAR REPLACES THE MARROW IN YOUR BONES...
YOU SERVED NOBLY, GOBLIN...
...BUT I DISCHARGE YOU FROM SERVICE. IT'S OVER.
GO INSIDE, NOW.
BUT ONE CONDITION REMAINS...
...AND YOUR SENSES STORM LIKE CYCLONES OUTSIDE YOUR BODY.
...TO PREVENT THE BLEEDING OF KAI-FANG-FU.

I LOVED HER SO.

IN THAT MOMENT, INEVITABILITY JUXTAPOSES WITH THE UNKNOWN...

...IN A FINALITY THAT'S SIMULTANEOUSLY TERROR...

THERE.

...AND RELIEF.

FOR ALL I HAVE BETRAYED, I MUST ATONE. I MUST SHOW YOU.

CANDI SNYDER, 1232 A.D.

Summer 2017:
SWAN SONG

SCISSOR SISTERS
CREATORS

Rich Perotta

Rich Perotta started as a freelance artist for many Marvel Comics for ten years in the late 90's before joing DC Comics on *Booster Gold* & *The Ray* in 2010. In 2013, Rich became the main artist for numerous independent titles including *Scales of Time* & *Scissor Sisters* for Inverse Press.

Erica J. Heflin

After years in independent film, co-creator & co-writer Erica turned to writing comics and enjoyed an extended run as writer of Zenescope's *Wonderland.* Her titles, *Antithesis* & *Flesh of White* are available through Inverse Press.

Kevin LaPorte

Co-creator & co-writer, Kevin hails from Fairhope, Alabama. He is publisher, editor & man-of-all-hats for Inverse Press. Other works include *Vicious Circus, Roadkill du Jour, The Absentee, Last Ride for Horsemen,* & *Scales of Time,* also with Rich Perotta.